For all who shepherd homeless dogs into furever homes,
and for those who choose to adopt rather than shop.
Tail wags to my editor, Emilia Rhodes,
and my agent, John Rudolph! – N.F.

To all the dogs I've ever loved – J.B.

First published 2019 by Houghton Mifflin Harcourt
This edition first published in the UK 2019 by Macmillan Children's Books
an imprint of Pan Macmillan,
20 New Wharf Road, London N1 9RR
Associated companies throughout the world
www.panmacmillan.com

ISBN 978-1-5290-1249-1

1 3 5 7 9 8 6 4 2

A CIP catalogue record for this book is available
from the British Library.

Printed in Poland.

NANCY FURSTINGER · JULIA BERECIARTU

The Duchess and Guy

A Rescue-to-Royalty Puppy Love Story

MACMILLAN CHILDREN'S BOOKS

Once upon a time,

a happy-go-lucky beagle named Guy found
himself without a family, or a place to call home.
He blinked his puppy dog eyes and wished that
someone would take him home.
But he didn't have much luck . . .

·Beagle
·Male
·Age: 3

. . . until he spotted Meghan and her pup, Bogart.

From the tip of his nose down to his toes,
Guy knew they would be a family.

Guy couldn't believe how lucky he was to have found Meghan, but Meghan always told Guy she was the lucky one.

One day, Meghan met her own match when she fell in love with a British prince named Harry.

Guy gave his paw of approval to Harry. He treated Meghan like the princess Guy always knew she was.

Soon, Meghan told Guy that they were going to move to a new forever home in England.

Guy couldn't wait to prove that he was a regal beagle at heart. For his grand entrance, he showed off his new dog trick: take a bow.

But the crown jewels the Queen wore dazzled him and he forgot which end should be up and which should be down.

Guy tucked his head into his paws.
He wasn't prim and proper like the Royal Family.

He and Bogart used to stir up all kinds of mischief back home.

As fun as their adventures were, Guy knew he would have to start behaving if he was going to fit in at the palace.

Could Guy help Lupo round up the royal children?

Guy tried to keep the successors in line, but instead he decorated the nursery with muddy paw prints.

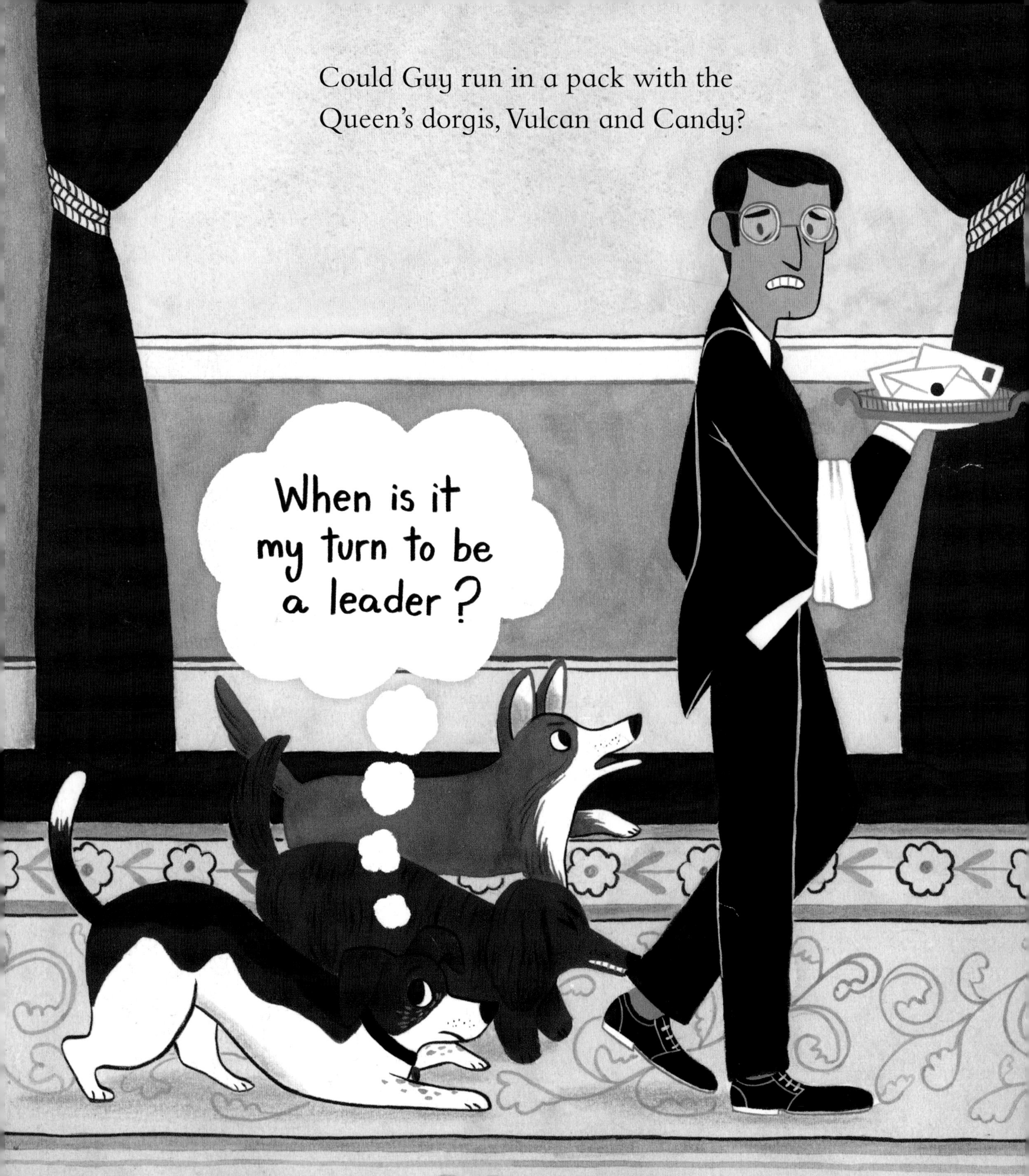

Could Guy run in a pack with the Queen's dorgis, Vulcan and Candy?

Guy tried to perk his ears up and get low enough to parade with their pack, but he didn't like how the dorgis were always bossing the humans around.

Could Guy join the Queen's Guard?

Guy tried to act tough, but the furry hat made him sneeze.

Finally, Guy thought he'd found his place serving tea.
He turned on his adorable beagle charm.

But his tail spun out of control.
Swish! Crash! Smash!
The Queen was not impressed.

Guy's ears drooped and the wag disappeared from his tail.
Every pup needs a purpose, but Guy couldn't seem to find his.

Even worse, Guy feared he
had disappointed Meghan.

Before Guy could woof an apology, Meghan gave him an encouraging scratch behind his ear.

"I wasn't sure I'd ever fit in here, either," Meghan told her pup. "But if you just be yourself, you'll be part of the family in no time."

Guy gave Meghan a big, sloppy beagle kiss.

Guy held his tail high. He knew just how to impress his new family now.

He would show them all of his and Bogart's old tricks!

One day, Guy spotted the Queen outside the palace. He still felt nervous around her, but when Guy looked the Queen in the eyes, he realized she had the same sad look that Guy got when he missed Bogart.

Before the Queen could turn away, Guy jumped into her car and sat beside her.

The beagle had waited for love before and now he'd wait until the Queen was ready to let him heal that dog-shaped hole in her heart.

Finally, Guy felt at home with his new family.
He never dreamt that his life would turn out this way back when he was wandering the streets homeless, trying to look like he belonged to someone.
Without a doubt, Guy knew he was the luckiest dog in the world.

You'll always be my best guy.

And together, they lived happily ever after.

Guy's True Rescue-to-Royalty Tale

In 2015, a lost little beagle was handed in to an after-hours kennel at the Montgomery County Animal Shelter, in Kentucky, USA. This shelter works closely with rescue groups to find new homes for unwanted animals. J'Rie Elliott, a volunteer at the time and currently the shelter coordinator, said that the dog was "a typical beagle, a bag of wags and giggles."

The shelter discovered that the poorly pooch tested positive for heartworm, a potentially fatal disease, so a local vet treated him and sent him to a foster home to recover. Once back to full health, a team of volunteers transported the pup 500 miles north to Ontario, Canada, where A Dog's Dream Rescue Centre promised to find him a forever home.

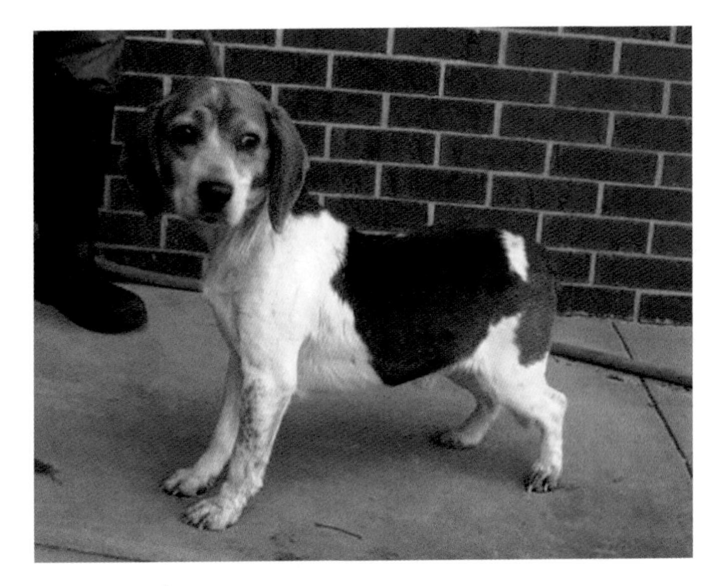

The seventeen-pound beagle was one of many homeless hounds at an adoption event held at Pet Valu, a Canadian pet store, in 2015. Meghan Markle had been searching for a friend for her dog, Bogart, a labrador-shepherd mix. He had been adopted from a dog shelter in Los Angeles after the TV host, Ellen DeGeneres, convinced Meghan that the pup was perfect for her.

Then Meghan spotted Guy. During a getting-to-know-you dog walk, Bogart approved of Guy and the two rescue dogs became the best of friends. Bogart and Guy lived with Meghan in Toronto, where the actress starred in the TV series *Suits*. Meghan called Guy and Bogart her "loves" and said the pair meant "the absolute world" to her.

Once Meghan and Prince Harry decided to move in together, Guy jetted off to London to join them. Meghan's vet advised her to rehome Bogart with close friends in Canada, as he was too old to make the long journey overseas to England.

Today, Guy lives at the palace with a black labrador puppy brother and is a much-loved and treasured member of the Royal Family.

Photos courtesy of J'Rie Elliott

Adopting a Dog Like Guy

Are you searching for a furry friend like Guy to offer a loving home to? There are loads of ways to find a new pet to adopt. Research rescue shelters and adoption centres in your local area online. From big to small, old to young, schedule a visit to meet *all* the different types of pups who are eager to find a forever home.

You'll have lots of choice. If you have your heart set on a purebred dog, such as a beagle or corgi, about a quarter of the dogs in shelters are pedigree. Or perhaps you'd prefer a one-of-a-kind marvellous mix, like the Queen's famous dorgis, a cross between a dachshund and a corgi.

When you adopt a dog, you'll be saving two lives: the life of your new pet and the life of another homeless dog who will fill the space in the shelter. There's no greater joy!